W9-BGB-236

THIS CANDLEWICK BOOK BELONGS TO:

To my brother, Ben
D. M.

For John F.
S. M.

First U.S. paperback edition 2000

The Library of Congress has cataloged the hardcover edition as follows:

Martin, David, date.
Five little piggies / stories by David Martin ; illustrated by Susan Meddaugh.
—1st U.S. ed.
p. cm.
Summary: The lines of a familiar nursery rhyme are expanded
into stories about the activities of a family of pigs.
ISBN 1-56402-918-2 (hardcover)
[1. Pigs—Fiction. 2. Family Life—Fiction.] I. Meddaugh, Susan, ill. II. Title.
PZ7.M356817Fi 1998 [E]—dc21 97-14667

ISBN 0-7636-1081-X (paperback)

2 4 6 8 10 9 7 5 3

Printed in Hong Kong / China

This book was typeset in Stone Informal.
The pictures were done in watercolor and ink.

Candlewick Press
2067 Massachusetts Avenue
Cambridge, Massachusetts 02140

Five Little Piggies

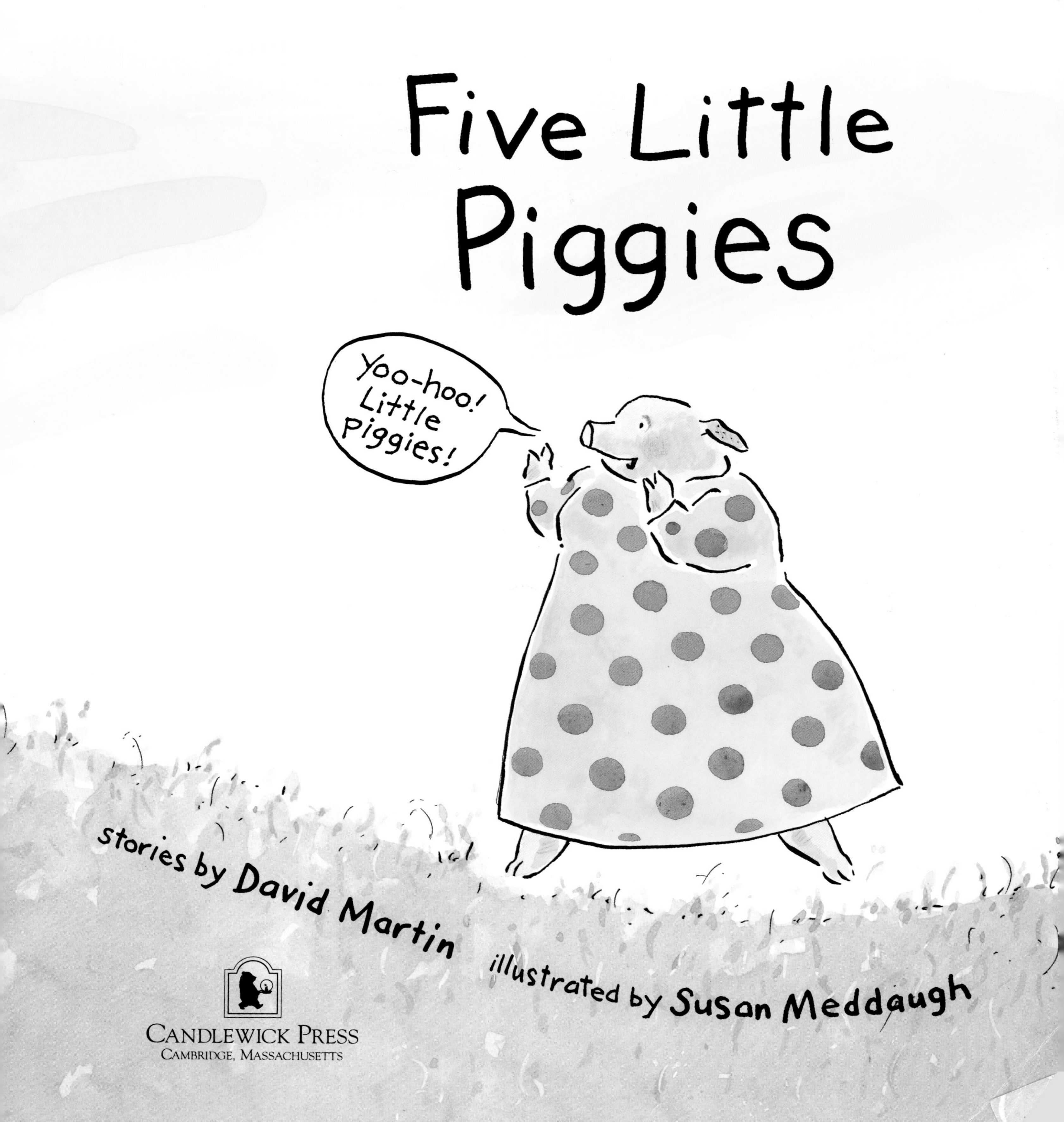

stories by David Martin

illustrated by Susan Meddaugh

CANDLEWICK PRESS
CAMBRIDGE, MASSACHUSETTS

1
This little piggy
went to market.
2
This little piggy
stayed home.
3
This little piggy
had roast beef.

4
This little piggy
had none.
5
And this little
piggy cried
wee wee wee
all the way
home!

1

This Little Piggy Went to Market

"Little Piggy, will you go to market? We need eggs and milk and apples," said Momma Piggy.

"Sure," said Little Piggy. And she went to market singing,

Eggs and milk and apples.

Megs and milk and mapples.

Pegs and pilk and papples.

When she got to the market she said,

On the way home she saw some chickens and cows eating apples.

"Oh, now I remember!" said Little Piggy, and she ran back to market and bought eggs and milk and apples.

"Mommy, I'm back," said Little Piggy.

"Good. Did you get everything?" said Momma Piggy.

"Oh, they're delicious pooples," said Momma Piggy.
"And here's a great big **BUG** for my silly piggy wiggy."

2

This Little Piggy Stayed Home

SPLASH!

Little Piggy spilled his juice.

CRASH!

He dropped his cereal on the floor.

RIP!

His pants split and
all the other little
piggies laughed
at him.

Momma Piggy said, “I think you should stay home with me today.” And she sent the others off to school.

All day long Little Piggy and Momma Piggy cooked and ate and played together.

"We had slopcakes and syrup for lunch!" said Little Piggy when the others came home from school.

The next day, all the other little piggies spilled their juice and dropped their cereal on the floor.

“Mommy, today can we stay home with you?” they asked.
“Of course you can,” said Momma Piggy.

“Not me,” said Little Piggy.
“I’m going to school.”

3

This Little Piggy Had Roast Beef

"Little piggies, come and eat," called Momma Piggy.

"Not slops again!" said Little Piggy. "Why can't we have roast beef?"

“Okay,” said Momma Piggy. “Here’s some roast beef.”

“It’s good, but something is missing,” said Little Piggy.

“Try it with some potatoes,” said Momma Piggy.

“It still isn’t right,” said Little Piggy.

“Here, dump in these bananas your brother sat on,” said Momma Piggy.

“Oh, that’s good,” said Little Piggy. “Can we put in the rotten eggs from breakfast, too?”

"Yummy!" said Little Piggy, and she threw in last week's soup and a squishy pickle.

"Now it's perfect. Try some, Momma!"

"Delicious!" said Momma Piggy.
"But it tastes like slops to me."
"No," said Little Piggy.
"That's not slops. That's
ROAST BEEF!"

4

This Little Piggy Had None

One day Momma Piggy went shopping and came home with treats for everyone.

But Little Piggy
dropped his
ice cream

and his
balloons
flew away

and then Little Piggy
had none.

Little Piggy cried and cried.

MOMMY!
I want
ice Cream!
I want
balloons!

Suddenly the other little piggies began to cry, too. And they cried even harder.

"Uh, oh. You four piggies all have chickenpox," said Momma Piggy. "But not you, Little Piggy. You have no spots, NONE!"

"Mommy! I **WANT** spots!" said Little Piggy.
"Okay," said Momma Piggy. "You can have spots, too."

5

This Little Piggy Cried Wee Wee Wee All the Way Home

Little Piggy was playing with the piggies next door.

Suddenly she got up and started running.
"Wee wee wee," she cried.

"What's the matter, Little Piggy?" asked her sister.

"Why are you crying?" asked her brother.

“Did you hurt yourself, Little Piggy?” asked Momma Piggy.
But Little Piggy just ran faster and cried,
“Wee wee wee,” all the way home.

Then she cried,
"Wee
wee
wee,"
all the
way up
the stairs.

And she cried, "Wee wee wee," all the way to the bathroom.

"OH!" said Little Piggy when she came out. "That felt good. I really had to go!"

DAVID MARTIN recalls that "my own children always asked me to play 'this little piggy,' except that the piggy who ate roast beef usually wanted pizza instead." David Martin is the author of *Little Chicken Chicken*, illustrated by Sue Heap; *Lizzie and Her Friend*, illustrated by Debi Gliori; and three other Lizzie picture books for toddlers.

SUSAN MEDDAUGH is the author and illustrator of *Martha Speaks* and *Martha Calling*, and is the illustrator of *Good Zap, Little Grog!* by Sarah Wilson, and other popular picture books. She says that once she figured out what Momma Piggy would look like, "everything else flowed. She's huge, but lighter than air, solid like a rock, yet buoyant. She's supermom!"
